"Your girlfriend and your cat, Seashell. What're you telling me?"

Her voice catches. "My girlfriend was in the living room. She said she'd just come from the bedroom, where my cat...."

"Seashell."

"Yes."

"What?"

"She said...she saw...Seashell...."

"Don't say it."

"No! She saw Seashell on the bed."

"The bed."

"Dead."

"The cat was on the bed, dead?"

"Yes."

"And your womb was erect."

"I want a child."

SHORTIES

TERRY HAYMAN

SHORTIES

fiero PUBLISHING

Published 2013 by Fiero Publishing
www.fieropublishing.com
Book and cover design copyright © 2013 by Fiero Publishing
Cover design by Terry Hayman/Fiero Publishing
Cover art copyright © 2013 soonwh/123RF Stock Photo

ISBN-13: 978-1927920039

ISBN-10: 1927920035

This is a work of fiction. All characters and events portrayed in this book are fictional and any resemblance to real people or incidents is purely coincidental.

First Print Edition: November 2013

COPYRIGHT ACKNOWLEDGEMENTS

"Erect" by Terry Hayman was first published in Stitches, May 2003

"Leptoid in My Ear" by Terry Hayman was first published by Fiero Publishing, March 2011

"Plague Poker" by Terry Hayman was first published by Fiero Publishing, November 2011

"The Rock" by Terry Hayman was first published by Grain, Fall 1988

"One Place" by Terry Hayman was first published by Fiero Publishing, February 2011

"Never Afraid" by Terry Hayman was first published by Fiero Publishing, November 2013

"Meant to Be Together" by Terry Hayman was first published by Fiero Publishing, January 2013

"Bad Cow" by Terry Hayman was first published by Fiero Publishing, November 2013

"Just One More Thing" by Terry Hayman was first published by Fiero Publishing, March 2011

"Toy Car Dialectic" by Terry Hayman was first published by Fiero Publishing, December 2011

Chasing the Minotaur by Terry Hayman was first publishing by Fiero Publishing, November 2010

For Bruce, my college roomie,
who loaned me his IBM PCjr
with which I typed the first
short story I ever sold.

SHORTIES

TABLE OF CONTENTS

Introduction

SHORT-SHORTS OR FLASH FICTION are usually considered stories under 1000 words. They may be passionate tales, comic riffs, or quiet meditations, but whatever they are, they're in and out of the idea or action really fast. Just enough time for you to take the whole story in a bite or two, then walk away slowly to digest it over time.

At their finest, it is my contention, they actually have a full three-act structure—set-up, exploration of the idea or theme (often with a try-fail sequence or two), and finally a payoff, an answer of some kind to the question or trouble that was raised in the opening. Not always a *solution* to that problem, mind you, but an answer. There have been trends in literary fiction to *not* finish the story. To merely present a slice of life and trust that the given slice is profound enough for the reader to draw their own conclusions.

Yeah. Um. That's not me. Usually. Life's inconclusive and confusing enough as it is. The fun thing about fiction is that we have a chance to give it structure and meaning. Which is why, I think, so many writers are either seekers of truth or convinced they've got bits of it and are eager to share.

After reading the stories in this collection, you'll probably conclude (correctly) that I plead guilty to being in both camps.

So how did these particular stories come to be?

"Erect" came to me in a dream. I literally woke up with most of this conversation in my head and a grin on my face. I gave it a bit of a framing device and punch line and somehow sold it to a magazine that I only discovered afterwards was for medical doctors sharing funny stories about their profession. Make of *that* what you will.

"Leptoid in My Ear" was written for a gambling magazine that folded before they could get to my story. Or maybe I made the magazine fold by sending it to them.

"Plague Poker" was me messing around (lightly) with divine intervention into the situation that was going on in the Middle East at the time.

"The Rock" was the first story I ever sold. Written as a break from studying law, it was mostly a chance to revisit in my imagination the wonderful lake I used to swim in at my grandparents' cottage in North Bay, Ontario.

I wrote "One Place" because I love painters and I love Paris. *Art Times* bought it and spread my love letter around. Years later, I channeled that love of painters and Paris into the much bigger canvas of my novel *Chasing the Minotaur.*

"Never Afraid" explores the theme of pushing ourselves (or being pushed by someone else) to face our fears.

"Asymptote", the title of which came from my mathematical son, is kind of SF, kind of infidelity fiction, but mostly it's about language. A gift for those of us who hear the words as we read them.

"Bad Cow" is a reworking of my longer story "Rough Cattle", just because.

Sticking in a lighter vein, "Limb Poker" was also written for that deceased gambling magazine, but is straight-out SF flash fiction.

"Just One More Thing" was a light-hearted spill of my greatest fears and wishes as a parent at the time I wrote it. Parenting ain't for the faint of heart.

And finally, "Toy Car Dialectic." Honestly, I have no idea where this one came from, but I do recall having a great deal of fun writing it. And reading it again, it still speaks to me. So, even though it's a little more challenging than some of the others, it gets to be the parting note of this collection.

Which gives you the skinny, *very* skinny, on these little pieces. Hope you enjoy them.

Terry Hayman
North Vancouver, BC
November 7, 2013

Erect

MEN. Women. Two different planets.

You want proof?

I'm flopped on my office couch, eating a greasy slice of pizza and fast-forwarding my surveillance video of Mr. I-can't-walk Phineas playing paintball, when the telephone rings. I stagger to my desk, round-file the pizza slice, and grab the receiver.

The voice on the phone is female - high and breathy, gasping almost.

"Hello?"

"Yeah?" I say.

"Help."

"What?"

"I'm erect."

"A wreck?"

"Erect. My womb is erect."

"Your womb is erect."

"And I'm hot."

"You got me hot."

"I just ran in with my womb erect, and my girlfriend...."

"Girlfriend?"

"And my cat, Seashell."

"Your girlfriend and your cat, Seashell. What're you telling me?"

Her voice catches. "My girlfriend was in the living room. She said she'd just come from the bedroom, where my cat...."

"Seashell."

"Yes."

"What?"

"She said...she saw...Seashell...."

"Don't say it."

"No! She saw Seashell on the bed."

"The bed."

"Dead."

"The cat was on the bed, dead?"

"Yes."

"And your womb was erect."

"I want a child."

"Ah?" I swivel 360 in my chair to help me follow the logic, and consider fishing my pizza slice out of the garbage. "There a boyfriend in the story?"

"I think he killed Seashell."

"Because...?"

"He couldn't get me pregnant."

"The boyfriend couldn't."

"Yes." She sobbed into the line and I pictured the girlfriend patting my caller's back.

"It's okay," I say.

Her voice firms. "You see, Steve was limp."

"When you were erect?"

"And desperate!"

"Ah."

"And there was a knock."

"A...knot?"

"Knock. On the door. It was Susan, my girlfriend."

"And Steve got upset."

"Horribly. He threw my clothes at me and I ran, crying, from the room, and out of the apartment."

"While your girlfriend entered."

"She watched me run. She called after me."

"And finally went inside."

"Yes! Steve was gone."

"How?"

"The fire escape."

"Ah."

"And she saw...she saw...."

"She saw Seashell on the bed, dead."

"Yes! Oh, God!" There's a thumping, wheezing sound as if she's thrown herself over the phone, weeping.

"Is there any blood?"

I hear a wheezing pause, a scraping. Then, "What?"

"On your cat. Ask your girlfriend to check and see if there's any blood."

"Ewww."

I hear the phone thump down, the broken noises of two females talking, a scuffle of feet receding.

Returning.

"Hello?" she says.

"Yes?"

"Never mind." A miaowing sound. Click.

She's hung up. I go for the pizza and brush off the pencil shavings that are stuck to it, but it's no good. Smells like kitty litter now.

You see? A woman wouldn't have gone after the chucked pizza.

Leptoid in My Ear

TALK TO ME," I whisper to the Leptoid.

"Pardon?" says "Doctor" Silver from her chair, spinning a glittering green pen in her fingers.

On the therapy couch I shake my head in frustration and point to my right ear.

"Oh," she says. Then she crosses her shapely legs, jots in her notebook, and waits with me.

"Tell me the odds," I whisper.

No response.

"Please?"

Silver interrupts. "What do you want it—"

"Him."

"—*him* to tell you the odds on, Mr. Olin?"

"Frank."

"All right. Frank."

I squirm so the couch leather squeaks under me. It's so soft it feels like it could rip. But Silver's not a real psychiatrist, I'm sure. More like a smart blond showgirl the casino downstairs has hired to *play* a psychiatrist with me. I'm not sure why, exactly, but I haven't had much choice in the matter.

She reaches over and touches my hand. "Frank? What would this friend in your ear tell you?"

I clear my throat. "Anything. He could give me the odds on you being...twenty-three. Estimate the cost of this couch. Whatever. But he won't talk to me now because I agreed to this psychiatrist couch thing. He doesn't like being called imaginary."

The pen moves in and out between her fingers. "Who called him imaginary? You?"

I shake my head and chew my lip. "Casino manager. Skinny chested guy with a gun in his suit. Said Lep was imaginary. That I was a card counter. He was going to throw me out."

"You don't think...Lep...is imaginary."

"I...." My mouth is suddenly dry. Hell. I roll

off the couch and begin pacing the room, finally wave my arms and face her. "Up until two months ago, I was nothing. A cook in a restaurant...."

"A chef?" She raises her sculpted eyebrows, impressed.

"Cook. Then this thing jumps into my ear and starts telling me things. Like which table's going to order which food. Actually,"—I wave my arms in exasperation—"which food probably. The odds, you know?"

The look of respect vanishes. Silver's eyes flick to her notes. "How do you know it's not just a voice, Frank? An hallucination?"

I bang my fists over my eyes. "First night, it says it'll jump out onto my pillow. So I get my magnifying glass and there it is!"

Silver quirks her head. "You could see it?"

"Barely," I pant, dropping my fists. "Just a dot. But moving so I'll know it's him. So I name him Leptoid. Like Lepton, you know? An elementary particle of existence. Really small."

"You don't think it was just your eyes?"

I blink and begin stomping around the room again. "I went to Reno and made six hundred thousand in four days before they kicked me out. Played the horses and made three hundred and fifty thou before I got bored. Slot machines, Pachinko, craps—all bad payoffs with sucky odds but I even did them and did okay. Finally came here. I made forty-five thousand this afternoon on blackjack!"

"Which is when they sent you up to me."

"Yeah." I run out of steam and come back to sit on the therapy couch facing her, our knees almost touching. "Why do that? Why not just kick me out?"

Silver shrugs and I'm suddenly aware of the smell of her—fresh peaches. And the way her breasts slide inside her grey silk shirt. The quick sound of her breathing. "Maybe to find out if they should worry about a Leptoid invasion," she smiles. "Or to shake your confidence in your own Leptoid. Maybe that's my job."

"Well they've certainly done that." I bite my lip and tap my temple over my right ear. "Lep? Lep? Come in, buddy. I'm dying here. Starting to think I'm psycho after all. *Lep?*"

Silver leans forward and presses a long, manicured finger to my trembling lips. "It's okay, Frank. Really. Let it go. With or without a Leptoid, you're still a very...special...man." Her lips follow her finger, then her body, the silk softness against my face, the buttons popping free. And I know she's doing it for the money, either the casino's or mine, but my hot-pumping blood doesn't care....

An hour later I'm thinking that these last two months crazy things have happened for me, you know? Why me?

Lying warm in the dark of Silver's office, her tousled hair resting on my naked chest, my hand strokes the plush carpet under us as I listen to her slow and steady breathing.

I ask Lep, "What were the odds, two months ago, I'd be sleeping with a Vegas showgirl and have a million bucks in my bank account?"

"*From your perspective, a zillion to one, Frank,*" Lep answers. "*From mine, a 78.57 probability. I chose you anyway. More of a challenge.*"

"Will they let me back into the casino downstairs?"

"*97% certainty. After this, they won't think you're dangerous. For a while.*"

"And...um...." I pause as Silver groans and shifts on my chest, her fingers unconsciously clutching my arm in remembered passion. "What are the chances 'Doc' Silver will sleep with me again?"

Lep has been in my ear long enough I swear I can sense his smile. *"Not really my field, Frank. But...I'd bet on it."*

Plague Poker

THE DEMON SKYXX SNEERED AT HIS ANGEL BROTHER, Oe, and looked down through the table. *"I've got Brillo-head. He's peeved at being passed over for promotion. Wants to cause a major biological incident without getting caught."*

Oe leaned over to see better. "My hand is the female?"

Skyxx grinned so that only his two needle teeth showed. "Dr. Hibe Binte Sulaymn. Trying to close the place down as unsafe. That's all I can get on her, though. She's one of yours."

"Yes." Oe nodded and sat back. "Your bid."

~~~~

Fahd blinked as if someone had suddenly energized his thoughts and body. The work of Allah, he thought. Making him strong for his destiny.

Beside him sat Hibe. In the fires of a western university she'd been tempted from her rightful place as man's consort and now served the Ayatollah as a sexless abomination. Thank Allah her womanly form was now concealed in the plastic-smelling biosuits they both wore. He would be glad when he was away from here and could picture the malignant pustules breaking out on her skin as—

"Watch it, Fahd!" she snapped at him, and Fahd saw that he had almost spilled the vial of anthrax into which he was squeezing a few drops of botulinum. This particular strain was far more persistent than those used in the Great Satan America, and consequently far more dangerous. Five spores alone could cling, multiply, become an entire jihad worthy of its makers.

Fahd smiled weakly at Hibe through his clear faceplate. Yes, she knew he struggled. She did *not* know he had already dummied the research logs and slipped two vials of the modified anthrax into a hidden pocket in his biosuit.

~~~~

"I bid Dr. Fahd's life," sneered Skyxx.

~~~~

Hibe shivered inside her suit as Fahd set the anthrax vial down, then gritted her teeth. She would never let this twisted man see how much he disturbed her. Letting someone like him work with such sensitive biological weapons was one reason she'd filed her initial report.

That report had been immediately burned by her superior, but what neither of the two other men running this research station knew was that she had sent a second report, complete with video and intra-country holocaust scenarios, directly to the head of the Islamic Labor Party who was a long-time family friend.

~~~~

What could Skyxx's human be planning? Oe wondered. And would he do it before Hibe's secret report was answered?

"See you with Dr. Hibe's life. Raise with five hundred women and children from the town of Mashhad, yours if Dr. Fahd prevails."

Skyxx spat. "See with the discovery of a hidden nuclear facility beside the Strait of Hormuz. Raise with the failure of a military coup being planned for November."

"See you with a stumble by the Freedom Movement."

~~~~

Twenty minutes later, peeled out of their suits and thoroughly decontaminated, Fahd followed Hibe out of the toxic lab. In his jacket pocket, the vial of anthrax seemed to squirm like a demon itself. A holy vengeance. All Fahd needed to do was sprinkle it into the building's ventilation system as he left early today on his vacation. Then all the betrayers in this compound who had denied him, their consorts, their families, they would never know what hit them. Day one: nothing. Day two: the onset of a common chest cold. Day three: blackened skin, raging abscesses, choking pneumonia, and finally...

"Many apologies, doctors," said the brusque, taut-skinned corporal who greeted them in their lounge area. "There will be no exiting the building today. It appears a UN Inspection Team has attained permission to pass through this area. Therefore we will be going on black status. We can risk no security breech."

Fahd went cold, his mouth sour. No exit. A possible inspection. "How long must we wait?"

The corporal shrugged and sniffed. "A day. A week. There is also a top priority response for you, Dr. Hibe." He handed her an envelope with a government seal.

Hibe opened it, hiding its contents from the men's eyes.

~~~~

"I bid a five year peace," Skyxx bluffed.

Oe raised ethereal eyebrows. "You have the power?"

Skyxx flashed the sign of his Master, held in reserve.

"Very well," said Oe easily. "I see and raise.

Twenty years of bloody civil war and despots if Fahd wins. You must call with twenty years of peace and democracy."

Skyxx studied Oe's face, as always that pure blue-white of Heaven. And, just maybe, the hint of a smile. Because of the Majles-e-Shura-ye-Eslami letter? Had Hibbe gone over her boss's head on this and won? Skyxx had nothing if she had. Fahd was a coward. He would panic and be discovered. Stopped. Then Skyxx would owe twenty years *of peace and democracy beyond all the other nonsense he'd offered?*

"I fold," Skyxx spat.

~~~~

The letter from General Ibrahim of the IRGC was curt and direct. Hibe was to keep to her place or be "released." The research facility was a valuable part of the Ayatollah's struggle for holy victory and would no more be compromised by rumblings within than by the fool UN Inspection Teams who would be shown no more than they were shown in Iraq.

Forcing a bemused smile onto her face, Hibe

folded it and put it into her lab coat pocket. Let Fahd worry a little.

~~~~

"You're not going to show me your hand?" raged Skyxx.

"You folded." With a smile, Oe reached down and stuck an invisible finger into the pocket of Fahd's jacket, touching the vial he'd suspected was there, rendering its contents inert. "For now, at least, the game is over."

The Rock

THE WATER WAS COLD AND DARK. He pulled through it with a listless breaststroke, letting it carry him. There was no one on the lake tonight. No campfires, trailer lights, human or animal sounds. No stars or moon, just clouds and night. Still water.

His T-shirt and underwear billowed then dragged as he gave a sloppy whip-kick. His feet felt numb and he sank them down under him to see. They were only a milky blur in the black water, so he plunged his face in and groped with his hands. Ah, he'd forgotten to take off his tennis shoes. Cold fingers fumbled blindly with the laces, then he kicked once, again, and cool water streamed around his toes. He pulled back up to the surface.

No moon, he thought, as he wiped water from his eyes. The thought slid out. He trod water. Then: Where's the rock? He turned a slow circle and found it, the uneven silhouette of the island. He blinked. The rock. He struck out again.

Pull, *sloosh,* water by his ears. Pull, *sloosh.* Pull, *Andy.* His brother, Frank, calling him Andy. Never Andrew. *C'mon, Andy.* Swimming out in dark like this once. Twenty yards. *Look, Andy, you can't see the campground.* Black universe under you. *Musky gonna get your toes.*

Sloosh.

A Chevvy screaming to death on a highway.

Musky got your toes, Frank.

~~~~

The island rose up, skewed off-center. The island. Where they ran around the shores and ducked into bushes for hide and seek. Where they jumped off the huge rock that jutted up the west side and dropped straight down through the water. *C'mon, Andy. How far down can you go before you have to come up?* Twenty-eight feet. The underwater avalanche there. His littel lungs bursting to live. *How far, Andy? C'mon!*

What shit. There was a rope down there.

Now the slowly turning silhouette of the island showed its bald west side and bumpy point. He plowed in low breaststrokes towards it, water rippling around his nose. His hair hung west in his eyes and his skin goosepimpled, but he didn't notice. As he approached, he slowed and his T-shirt billowed up under his arms and around his chest. A bubble wiggled its way up from under him and popped to the surface. He turned on his back and started to kick his way in to the point. But I'll hit my head, he thought, so he stopped. He sunk his middle and turned.

And there was the rock.

The pitted face rose in front of him to a dry height of six or seven feet, climbable only around its right side. But he wasn't going up. He gauged the center of the rock, scraping his body against it. Then he faced outwards, sucked an involuntary breath, and dove.

How far down...

The surface water had seemed cold and the

air chill, but only four feet down, he plunged through a doorway of ice. And every four feet after that, another doorway. His mind pushed his body down and down, through cold and lungs shrinking to gasp at the cold and pressure. His ears popped once, and again. Then, in the blackness, he found the avalanche and started groping over rocks and slime.

Rocks. Big rocks some underwater demon had kicked up around the feet of *the* rock that dared raise its head above the surface. One of the lesser rocks had a rope around it, tied and wedged, with a free end that had once reached up to the surface, held erect by an empty, sealed plastic gas tank. He and Frank had tied it, rigged it as a way down to explore the depths. Years ago. The gas tank was gone but he knew the rope was still here, lying thick, limp, and tied down out of sight.

...before you have to come up?

The oxygen in his lungs was going, eaten greedily by his blood, but then his fingers found the rope. Slimy and long, it ran through his hands as he blindly pulled up a length and wrapped it around his leg. The knot he tied was a simple granny repeated twice then three times, his fingers working faster as his lungs started to cry. Then he shot upwards, his body struggling for life in spite of him, and the knots tightened with a jerk. His arms pulled at the water, reaching up and ripping down through a blackness his eyes could not burst but his whole body could feel. Each muscle aware and struggling and feeling, but held by some *thing* grabbing at his leg. His body struggled frantically but the *thing* would not let go.

It's killing me. It won't let go. IT WON'T LET GO!

His fingers reach down to the rope.

Stay calm!

The fingers pry, loosen, twist, pull and the mind directs them. Please God, oh please God oh please!

The lungs rip and pull the throat in and out spastically, demanding it open for air. Two knots undone, and the skin of an ankle the eyes can't see is torn bloody by hemp and scratching fingers. And the body wants to leap and break the rope or leave the leg behind.

The mind shoves the fingers at the last knot. The knot comes free. The body pulls for the surface, with popping eardrums and bend-wrenching cramps as nitrogen bubbles out of the blood.

~~~~

Andrew broke the surface with a gasp to suck in stars. He couldn't see past the blood and cramping guts, but his arms beat frantically to keep him on the surface. Finally, the red receded, and he realized he now saw the night, not death. His arms slowed. A few seconds later, he pulled towards the right of the rock.

In the darkness he found the shallow slope of the low hard ledge he and his brother used to sit on after a dive. He pulled himself up and lay trembling, breath rasping. His legs twitched and would not stop, but he forced his body straight and worked a fist into his stomach cramps. Twenty minutes of absorption in pain and his head was clear again. He noticed for the first time there were stars between some of the clouds, and there was a slight breeze. He shivered, then pulled himself up, shaking, on the ledge. Barefoot in dripping underwear and T-shirt. He stripped them off and climbed onto the big rock, standing naked and looking out at the lake and sky.

"Goodbye, Frank."

A rush of air and night filled his lungs.

Whatever it takes, Andrew. Whatever it takes.

One Place

MADELINE BACKED UP CAREFULLY near the sooty bricks. Nose twitching at the stench of un-collected garbage, she double-checked her map then craned her neck up to read the street plaque on the wall. Looked back to her Paris map. Up again. Back. Annoyed.

What artist would take a bet to confine himself to one of these little streets for fifteen years? These weren't the artist stalls of *Place du Tertre* or the twisting streets of *Montmartre*. This was narrow, West Bank dinge. What possible reason...?

"*Pardon*," she coughed in tortured French, reaching out to the laborer passing by. He shrugged her off and kept walking. To another she called "*Pardon, le painteur? L'artiste?*"

That one pointed down the street without breaking stride.

"*Merci!*" she called after him, realizing it sounded like *Mercy!* Certainly what her feet needed, she thought, as she set off again in her pumps.

Then, rounding the indicated corner, she saw him. He sat slouched on a stool on the narrow sidewalk, easel and canvas in front of him, a little slug of a man with a self-cut rag of mouse-brown hair, a chin of stubble, and twitching, paint-stained fingers.

As Madeline watched, two women casually stepped onto the street to walk around him. He was an accepted fixture. He would have to be if the story of painting here for fifteen years was true.

"Charlie Samuels?" Madeline said, approaching slowly.

The slug's eyes jerked up at her, then back to his picture as if he wondered how she could exist if she weren't on the canvas.

"Mr. Samuels." Madeline glanced at her watch, at the distracted man before her, and decided to lay it out bluntly. "I'm a New York art dealer. I've sought you out because I might want to represent you. Your work, the ones that made it to America, they show the promise of a new Van Gogh."

His fingers stopped twitching. For a long moment there was silence. Then, without looking up, he whispered, "But...?"

Madeline tilted her head. "I have to know your early collection wasn't a fluke. When I invest in a painter, I invest in his whole life. I take him to New York. I build his career. So I need to understand *why you are here.*"

There was a long, tense pause. Then he choked out, "You need to understand?"

"There are stories of a bet. Of you agreeing to live just on this street. To never leave it until you're a success. Why would you agree to that?"

Another long silence during which the man struggled for breath and the smell of his sweat rolled from him like an octopus squirting ink. Finally he set down his brush and looked up at her. The pain in his grey eyes rolled out even more powerfully than his smell. "When I was eighteen, I ran away from Harvard Business School to be a painter here. Paris." He took a breath and the words spilled out faster. "My father tracked me down, though. Told me I didn't know what I was doing. I said I did. That I'd do anything to be a painter. So my father laughed and made me a bet. He said he'd keep supporting me financially *if* I could stay in one place long enough to make a success of my art. I accepted the bet and put down my foot here. Right here on this street." He feelingly stabbed an ochre finger at the sidewalk.

Madeline let out a slow breath. "I don't believe you. Why take the bet?"

"I wanted to paint."

"Surely it would be better to be poor and *free*."

"And a failure?" Samuels looked up with those eyes Madeline knew would soon grace the cover of the *New York Art Review*. But not from his travels, she now understood. Even though he had won his bet and was free, the way his hand had frozen on his paintbrush when she'd talked of New York, the passion that swept his voice when he spoke of "this street"—they said he was never going to leave. Madeline would have to market his work from here and make his incredible story part of his mystique. As if to confirm it, Samuels said, "Art exists wherever you are. If I couldn't find it here, I knew I wouldn't find it anywhere else either."

She shook her head. "It was an absurd bet."

"No. Because I knew I would win."

"How?" she exploded.

"A question of the stakes," he said. "You see, my father is rich and he has two other sons, so he gambled simply what he could *afford to lose*." The painter turned back to his street, took up his brush, and tilted his head with a wistful smile. "I gambled my whole life."

Never Afraid

WILLIAM STOOD RIGHT TO THE EDGE OF THE ROOF, his worn oxfords poking over. The frayed bottoms of his pants flapped in the wind. He felt sweat staining the little armpits of his seersucker.

A gust of wind made him shoot his arms to out for balance. His soft jaw dropped to his chin.

"You see all right, then?" said Margritte, well back.

"W-wonderful," said William. He took an exaggerated breath and brought his hands in to slap his chest. That almost unbalanced him and made him shoot the arms out again.

"See the other roof?"

William looked down and swallowed. Across

the narrow alley, the next roof was maybe twelve feet away, ten feet lower than this one. "Piece of cake."

"You'll need a run."

"You?"

She shook her head. "This is just you, Billy."

William hesitated. Margritte was thirty-six. Unmarried. A nasal voice and disappearing lips. The kind of woman most men didn't look at twice.

"You're not scared, are you? We could just go back downstairs. Coffee break's almost over."

She dug a cigarette out of her purse, lit it, and sucked so the end of it shone red. William coughed. His throat was dry; his legs, wobbly. She took the cigarette out of her mouth, almost sympathetic.

"Done much jumping?" she said.

William shook his head. "Back in school. You know...."

"Long time ago."

"Not so long."

She smiled. "Well then."

William swallowed and tried to calculate the jump, but he'd never been good at math, even as a school kid, running pell-mell down steep hills with friends, climbing out after curfew, going everywhere. Never afraid.

But now he had a pudge around his middle. His arms were little keyboard-punching spindles. His knees were knobs that clicked on cold, wet mornings.

And Margritte was waiting.

"Right." William inched back from the edge, took three long strides back, looked again, took another five.

Margritte flicked the ashes of her cigarette, arms folded across her chest.

He ran.

His foot shoved him off the edge so hard he flew off-balance. Wind rushed past his ears. Cellophane and dirty papers rustled far below. His arms clawed through space to...

Whack the other roof edge.

They bounced off. Grabbed.

Held.

Then through the giddy pounding in his ears, acid in his fingers and arms, William fought for his life. *Up.* How much did he weigh now? Two hundred pounds? *Up!* Couldn't do a pull-up in the gym.

But now his fingers gripped like steel hooks and his flabby arms pulled like sweating, desperate thick rubber bands up and over the rough edge of the rooftop.

His upper torso cleared and flopped down. His right knee followed. He rolled over and wept. Finally he rose and staggered backwards so he could see onto the roof where Margritte had watched.

She was gone.

Later, he asked her, "Did you see?"

She shook her head and kept typing, but William knew she admired him now.

Asymptote

I N A DIMENSION CLOSE TO OURS sits a woman at a table. On the table is a plate. On the plate is a marble. It's not glass or made of steel. It's of smooth, hard flesh like all our lives are packed and rolled and pressed together there.

It is us.

Us?

No. You.

It is your life the woman rolls around and around, using her fingers as soft little goads, the edges of the plate as edges of your world. Psychic edges. Scary places.

With every goad you roll and spin, your breath comes in, your eyes fly wide…

~~~~~

"Marion? My goodness, I didn't see you there. Must be distracted today. The Graybill account. Working hard on... What's wrong?"

"Mr. Archer, I'm...sorry...I'm..."

"Call me Bob. Please. Are those tears? I... Look, why don't we just step into my office here and... That's better, isn't it? Now just tell me what... Oh my goodness. Alright, I'll hold you a second. There there."

"No! I can't do this! I'm sorry. I'm so so sorry!"

"Marion?"

"I can feel my heart beating. So hard!"

"I can feel it too."

~~~~~

Her breath is warm, the woman at the table. Her fingers soft. Her laugh jingles through the ether as she spins you by the edge...

~~~~~

"You're married!"

"Yes, I am. I don't… Oh, dear. Marion. Ms. Pietro. No, now don't get the wrong idea here."

"Don't push me away! I know I'm not wrong! I've seen it in your eyes for weeks. Months. Forever. Everybody in the office knows. They all think we're already together."

"No, now, um…hum… Everyone… That's not good. That's not right."

"It is! It is exactly right!"

~~~~~

The table woman rolls you, heart in throat, back the other way…

~~~~~

"Bob. Oh, Bob, I'm sorry."

"No, me. Of course, me. Things in my heart, perhaps. In my thoughts. I don't know. But it could never… I could never…"

"I know. I know. Now. I know. I'm so sorry. So embarrassed."

~~~~~

And who's been rolled? the woman laughs. The He or She? The plate is served, the surface slick. Upon it we just roll and spin. It's you to me, or me to you, or we to whom?

While on we spin…

Bad Cow!

THIS MONEY'S FOR YOU, MA'AM. You see....

First there was a stampede. It ran the cattle into this keyhole canyon where we finally stopped them. Set up camp. But the cows and steers looked plumb run out, straggly and thin.

So that night, me, Boss, and Cook, are sitting round this crackle-pop fire, laying money down on how many cattle we're going to lose, when two of our *vaquero* come over. One's your husband, Chico, and he slaps his whole moneybag down. Says, "We lose all of them."

Cook snorts. "We're two days to railhead. Is this Mexican boolshit?"

Chico farts and turns to the other *vaquero*. "Tell him."

47

The other *vaquero* is called *La Mesteño*, the mustang, because he's got this broad leather belt with silver buckles, a buckskin jacket with silver buttons, broad hat, oiled mustache, and a lariat he likes to practice with when we ride. Real neat. Real serious. He lowers his head and says with a heavy accent, "The stars fall."

Boss frowns. "What?"

Chico says, "Last night, before the rain stops, we see lights flash in the sky."

La Mesteño says, "And they come down... there."

He's pointing into the middle of our herd where they're huddled against the canyon wall. And we suddenly hear some bellowing sounds from in there. We stand up. And beat it if three longhorn in the center aren't tossing about and goring the cattle around them.

Boss says to me, "Bud, you and *La Mesteño* get those three and we'll dehorn 'em."

So we saddle up and ride into the herd and our horses almost trip over these burnt-looking scorches in the earth. Where the stars fell? But we get the three longhorn out and rope them to two trees by Cook's wagon.

The three are rolling their wild eyes at us, and we're about to saw their horns, when Cook says, "Stop." He holds a lantern down near their bellies. They got big festering ulcers or something there that we can smell now. Almost chokes us.

"Maggots," mutters Cook, who's also the drive doc, and goes to his wagon. Comes back with his mix of carbolic acid, axle grease, and stuff. Stinks worse than the ulcers.

"Hold that one," he says, and three of us do as Cook slathers on the stuff.

The steer gives this unholy screech and bucks loose, then falls over dead, his stomach rippling and bulging where I guess the maggots are. We all jump back with guns out, and when the wormy things burst onto the grass, so many guns shoot them they're just bits and blood.

Then the other tied longhorn rear up on their hind legs and kick at Chico. He tries to duck but their hooves smack his forehead, killing him, poof.

Right sorry, Ma'am.

So we shoot those two longhorn too and they fall over, thump. No wriggling in their bellies. We're watching, sweaty palmed and pumped.

And just when we're about to let out our breaths, those two dead steer suddenly twitch, scramble to their feet, and regard us calmly with these black-and-red-shot eyes. We back away, scared, and the two longhorn amble slowly back to the herd.

"Shit," says Boss. "Ain't no one gonna buy those two at the railhead."

After burying Chico and the dead steer who stayed dead, we sit around the campfire and make a new round of bets. Boss now figures with this infection we might have to kill off a third of the herd. Cook figures half and I say more. *La Mesteño* says, "We should kill them all. Or we die."

Like I said. Serious.

Then, just before morning, *La Mesteño* shakes me awake to yell, "Get on your horse!" Because the herd, it's stumbling, all red-and-black eyed, straight for the camp. Then it breaks and stampedes for us, but me and *La Mesteño* are in the saddle and ride out of the way. And he's riding no-hands, carrying these big watering cans, one in each hand.

"Kerosene!" he shouts, and hands one over, mid-gallop. "We burn them!"

So we gallop in circles around the rampaging cattle, sloshing on the kerosene. Then we veer in by the campfire and each scoop up a firebrand. Sling it out into the herd.

Whoof! Crackle!

Crispy cow!

And we keep shooting and burning them till we're out of kerosene and bullets. Then we ride like hell with a bunch of the herd chasing us. Get here.

Then....

Well, then you waved, Ma'am. And me and *La Mesteño*, we decided the money's rightfully yours. Take it.

But...you say my husband bet all the cattle would die.

Yup. They're all dead.

And that shrieking from the edge of town?

That's them. And whatever's driving their flesh now. Figure it'll be spreading soon. Which is why, begging your pardon, me and *La Mesteño* are getting a lo-o-o-ng way out of here.

So good day to you, Ma'am.

God bless.

Limb Poker

T WAS JUST HIM AND THE KRITA'AN, with Elias down two arms and a foot. But Elias was lucky. The Krita'an wanted all of him.

Tapping its claws on the table now, drool spilling from its mandibles, the Krita'an waived Elias's ante. The watchers in Zarn's IG Pub grunted smells of anticipation.

The Krita'an hissed and the table box translated it to, "Your deal."

Elias fingered the deck of cards. He'd beaten the Geldan to his right by reading the fur twitch at its throat. He'd also tagged the Mona to his left and eased her out of the game before she lost any body parts. But the Krita'an—its face was insect, the eyes huge and mirrored. Elias couldn't read it at all.

"I will enjoy drinking your intestines," it hissed.

"And everything in them, no doubt." Elias fanned, snapped, shuffled, let the Krita'an cut, then dealt. Five cards. Draw poker. And Elias had...almost nothing.

Pair of threes. A queen. He looked at the side-to-side of the Briata'an's mandibles. A signal?

Elias's bid. "What will it take to get back my arms and foot?"

A hiss. "Your legs."

"I bet my legs."

"Call with your arms and foot. Raise 5,000 bola."

"Call with...my buttocks?"

"Agreed."

"How many cards?"

"Two."

His guts a hard lump of ice, Elias gave the Krita'an two and dumped the Queen to take three himself. Another pair – Jacks. Two pair, then. If the Krita'an had even three-of-a-kind, Elias was a quadruple amputee with no ass.

Unless he took it further.

"My liver and kidneys," he bet. These, like most human body parts, were mechanically replaceable on earth's mercy plan. Sucky replacements, of course.

"Match with 5,000 bola," the Krita'an hissed. The Mona and Geldan howled. "I mean 50,000. Raise 100,000."

"Match with...my yummy intestines?" The Mona and Geldan grunted approval. "Raise you one lung." Both replaceable.

"Match 50,000. Raise 500,024."

Silence around the table.

"This is all my money," hissed the Krita'an.

Elias finally said, "What do you want?"

"Your heart and brain."

Not replaceable.

Elias stared at the creature. A Krita'an with no bola was fertilizer. Would it risk that or was it a bluff? Elias sniffed the Krita'an's fetid breath, studied the eyes, the limbs, the mandibles.

And saw something new.

"I bet," he said slowly, "my heart and brain." And therefore my life.

A beat, then the Krita'an turned over its cards. Two jacks. One measly pair. Elias let his blank mask crack as he turned over his own winning hand.

The Krita'an's mandibles froze, a known pre-attack gesture, but three Zarn bouncers crashed in through the door. The Krita'an looked from them to Elias. "Another hand?" it hissed.

Elias snorted and reached for the Krita'an's bola card.

~~~~

Later in the bar, Elias felt a bump behind him and the Mona's sharp nails on his arm. "Tell me," she said in bad Standard. "You knew the creature was bluffing. How?"

Elias smiled. "Ah, it wanted to eat me, you see. All that drooling and mandible clicking."

"Hunger signs."

"Well, after it got its last cards and saw it had nothing...."

"Yes?"

"Its drool stopped."

Just One More Thing

CHARLES PETER CROSS GERALD WENTWORTH FARTHING SMITH was supposed to be named just "Charley Smith."

Until Charley's mother *insisted* on the Peter. Charley's father then *demanded* the Cross. They both agreed he needed a Gerald. Wentworth had been in the family for generations. And that should have been that. But when Charley's mother said, "So, we're done then?" Charley's father said...

"Just one more thing." And he added the Farthing.

All well and good. Charley was a cute baby who giggled a lot. The many names seemed to hang off him like feathers off a rainbow.

Unfortunately, he was so cute that when it came time to dress him for his first outing, both his mother and his father *had* to be involved. His mother put on his quilted diaper and shirt. His father chose the designer coveralls and bib. His mother selected the socks and authentic Indian moccasins. His father picked out the sunglasses and hat and red ribbon for his neck. And that should have been that.

But as Charley's father proudly said, "So, we're ready to go?" Charley's mother said...

"Just one more thing." And she added a sun umbrella so frilly Charley was quite hidden from view.

This, for Charley's sake, was also well and good.

When Charley turned five, his father carried his knapsack for him to the front door of the kindergarten. His mother helped Charley put the knapsack on. Both took his hands and walked him into the classroom, and introduced themselves to the teacher, and ensured his jacket was stored where he could find it, and carefully examined the floor for dust or sharp objects as they prepared to leave. But when the teacher said, "I'm glad that is that," Charley's parents both held up a finger and said together...

"Just one more thing."

Then they grabbed Charley by his hands, sang him the potty song in front of everyone, and walked him down the hall to go pee before school.

Charley did not think this well and good at all.

But though Charley wished more and more often that his parents could do one *less* thing, it was not to be. So Charley tried to anticipate.

The time his family moved neighborhoods, he warned his new friends to expect visits and thank you's for choosing him to like. These came...*and* a new bicycle for each friend so he or she could go riding with Charley. When he gobbled his meal down broccoli first to avoid a "healthy heart" lecture, he received the expected applause...*and* his parents plunged him into a new vitamin and exercise regimen based on the latest medical research. On his thirteenth birthday, Charley tried showing them a list of the books he planned to read, knowing they would forbid half the titles and substitute their own alternates. They did...*and* not only demanded book reports for each but insisted he write his *own* novels. With their help of course.

Finally, when at his high school graduation his parents, in front of the entire graduating class, presented him with around-the-world travel tickets to "get a global perspective" before tackling the university they'd gotten him accepted at, Charley lost his temper.

"Enough!" he yelled so loudly that the entire room of graduates and their families turned to watch. "You have loved me *too much!* You have tried *too hard!* You have gone *too far!* I have had it! As of today I cut my ties to you! I make my own decisions and plot my own future! You will not help me, hinder me, control me, dress me, direct me, depress me, or even *eject* me! *I* do it! *Me!*

"LEAVE...ME...ALONE!!"

He whacked the tickets to the floor in the hush of the auditorium, glared at the crowd and began stomping through the cleared pathway to the exit. Stopped.

"Just one more thing," he said. Charley turned and smiled. "I love you both very much. Always have. Always will."

And that, at least, his father and mother thought with beaming smiles, was well and good indeed.

Toy Car Dialectic

WHEN HE WAS SEVEN, Boris Sapersky wanted a Hot Wheels set that had lots of track, a loop-de-loop piece, and a way to make his Hot Wheels cars jump.

It satisfied his need, his mother and father believed, to experiment with spacial geometries and classic Newtonian physics—specifically the principles of speed, inertia, and the dispersion of energy when objects collide.

By the time he was nine, he had graduated to powered, remote controlled units, which usually had oversized wheels, penis-envy designs in lime green and fantasy purple and could be taken out-side to jump medium-sized muddy ditches with a properly-built jump and long enough run-up.

His father decided this probably indicated a future in rocket science or at least mechanical engineering. Boris's mother, who had sunk into a pattern of depression and extramarital affairs, figured it meant Boris was gay or emotionally retarded.

"How often does he go over to someone's house?" she asked.

"Less often than you," her husband said.

When Boris turned twenty-one and graduated from Cal-Tech with a degree in plant system computer modeling, he landed a job with a farm conglomerate which had a goal of replacing its entire crop rotation with genetically modified species designed to grow year round with bigger yields and more pest resistance. It was Boris's good fortune that the company was bought out by a fertilizer concern in his first year working there. Boris's converted stock options not only let him put a down payment on a house, but let him buy a cute little Mazda Miata, dandelion yellow. Its cheerful appearance and Boris's apparent financial success attracted numerous young women, one of whom, Gillian Joshi, not only taught him the ways of the *Kama Sutra*, but also got him marching down the aisle.

Their honeymoon was spent driving through Mexico in the Miata, getting very drunk in the many cheap bars, and being robbed of their passports and all their money on a pristine beach on the Baja Peninsula.

At thirty-seven and feeling straightjacketed by a medical services biotech company in which, as one of forty-nine vice-presidents (and not one of the ones pulling in six figure bonuses), he no longer did direct research, Boris was head-hunted by a Utah-based start-up that was trying to reclaim deserts in both the U.S. and Africa. He accepted, but Gillian, who had modeled her married life on Boris's mother, had far too much invested in her west coast affairs. As they'd never had children and Gillian had been as successful in her field of fashion retail and Boris had been in biotech, they parted amicably with promises of exchanging divorce papers..

Boris used his signing bonus to buy himself a Chevvy Corvette in midnight blue with a cherry red fender and spoiler to drive to Utah. He picked up a beautiful redheaded hitchhiker just outside Elko, Nevada, had sex with her in a Utah gas station, got the clap, and spent his third week on the job running a high fever and having delusions he was an Indy 500 race car driver, though not top seeded. The redhead, it turned out, was a transsexual and Boris bumped into her years later in a Salt Lake City bar. She enticed him into sex once again (but Boris wore a rubber this time), and referred him to her therapist for what Boris was recognizing was a fixation on cars as personality substitutes. He'd gone through eight since he'd moved to Utah as he was having trouble reconciling his Mormon workplace culture, the beatnik vibe of the neighborhood he'd settled in, and his own hedonistic impulses.

At fifty-five, though, he seemed to have it all worked out. He'd become a radical environmentalist and had started up a string of waste-conversion plants in California, Oregon, Illinois, and New York. His daily commuter car was a blood-red Tesla Roadster, all electric, zero to sixty in under four seconds, and he was financing a former Tesla employee in the race to build all-electric multi-passenger airplanes and pleasure boats.

When rolling electrical blackouts began hitting California again in the summer of Boris's fifty-seventh year, Boris took it as a sign that even his Roadster and M77 twin-motor electric speed-boat were not acceptable before God. He sold his businesses and vehicles, and began a decade-long quest to build a self-sufficient retreat on one acre of arid land that was powered entirely by solar and wind power, sustained through clever crop rotations, and connected to the outside world via a human-powered three-wheeler that Boris could push up to sixty miles per hour on a flat stretch of desert, with a bit of helpful tailwind.

Needless to say, female (and male) groupies flocked to the iconoclast's estate, many staying for the night, one particularly enthusiastic blond lasting an entire month before she realized Boris really had little money left and few interests beyond his crops and his HPV.

This final identity brought him to his seventies when his wife Gillian, who, like Boris, had never gotten around to sending or signing any divorce papers, came out to get him and bring him to live with her in a retirement village in San Diego.

Gillian had lived common law with a nice older Hawaiian businessman for almost twenty-five years after splitting with Boris. And though her Hawaiian was dead, she'd had two children by him, and now regularly entertained five grandchildren, off and on, in her three bedroom townhouse. She kept a well-stocked toy box in the guestroom just for them, filled with, among other childhood delights, a cornucopia of toy cars and bits of track, jumps, electric accelerators and toy car washes, even a make-believe ethanol fueling station.

When Boris saw this, he wept. For he finally understood, in watching Gillian get down on her knees with these cars and her grandsons and granddaughter the very day she brought Boris back with her, what it was to be truly loved. And that it was this love, not the cars, which he had been pursuing all his life.

The next day, when Gillian woke up beside him for the first time in thirty-six years, she found Boris dead, one hand on her breast, the other clutching a small, orange-and-purple Matchbox racer.

She pried both hands loose with a shiver of disgust and called the mortician she'd used to bury her Hawaiian. The man smiled when he saw her, anticipating the same sweet exchange of services as last time. But when he saw Boris's repose, something melted in his fatty old heart.

"I'll cremate him for free," he said, "if I can keep the ashes."

Gillian frowned at him, not sure if she should be offended. "Why?" she asked.

"I'm not sure," he said. He stroked Boris's claw-shaped hand. "Somehow he reminds me of better days."

Afterword

I T ALL ENDS TOO SOON, doesn't it?

Simple solution—go and pick up another collection where you got this one. Or one of my novels, *Chasing the Minotaur* or *Jessica Falls.*

Thanks for reading. And may your days be filled with so much life that your dreams are fuller and richer than any fiction could ever be.

-Terry

ALSO BY TERRY HAYMAN

Chasing the Minotaur

Jessica Falls

Raised by a Vampire

Being Human (collection)

Off World (collection)

Dark Paths (collection)

Life Knots (collection)

Messed Up (collection)

Used by Magic (collection)

Vamp (collection)

You can find more information about Terry Hayman and his writing at *www.terryhayman.com*. To purchase these and titles by other authors, please visit *www.fieropublishing.com*.

Keep reading for a sample from Terry Hayman's novel about an acclaimed New York painter who visits the south of France with his daughter to deal with the loss of his wife and discovers an olive grove where the long-dead painters Picasso, Renoir, Cézanne, and Van Gogh mysteriously still walk and paint, scheme and love.

CHASING THE MINOTAUR

Terry Hayman

1

A girl from the street

The young woman slipped from the snowy honking and bustle of Manhattan's evening rush hour, into the Hebbler Gallery on Wooster Street. As the thick door closed behind her, all the clatter from the street outside *hushed*.

It so startled the teen that Max Hebbler, watching from softly-mumbling crowd in the south atrium, thought she might drop to her knees in a primitive reflex.

She did not, thank goodness. But she did reach back one black-gloved hand to steady herself on the door frame. With her other hand, she pulled off her purple ski hat and stuffed it into the pocket of her dirty red bomber jacket. For another moment she stood very still, eyes fixed, long died-black hair half-covering her face. Max wondered if she worried about her boots tracking in the dirty slush from the sidewalk outside. Or if she looked at the other patrons and art lovers standing in small groups before the carefully-arranged paintings of artist Emery Lake and saw how out of place she was. The clothes, the excessive black eyeliner, the attitude.

Yet even as Max allowed himself the unchari-table hope the girl would turn and leave, the girl shook back her hair. Max took an involuntary breath and his old heart jumped.

Mein Gott. The hair. The little chip nose.

It was Lyssa.

No. Of course it was not Lyssa because Lyssa had been dead what? Eighteen years? Yes. Eighteen years, forty-three days, a handful of hours. The hours, Max could not know because he had not been there when his daughter died. He had only the coroner's estimate.

But...*mein Gott.*

Max ran his hand over his face. It was the light, of course. The winter light outside had been strange all day, shifting from silver gray to boiling pitch. And even though the gallery had its own carefully controlled lighting, especially for the showing of these paintings, the narrow windows to the street let in just enough of the outside strangeness that the front room felt infused with spirits.

Perfect for an Emery Lake showing.

The girl, still hesitating, had let some of her nonchalance crumble and now seemed clenched in fear. Following the direction of her gaze, Max saw she was staring at the signs pointing to the north atrium where, in just under an hour, Max would be sliding the front off a specially-constructed crate containing the most recent, and possibly last ever, painting that Max's star artist had completed.

Did the girl know Emery? Was that it? Was there a final piece of the story Emery had not told him?

Or was there...something else?

Even as Max decided impulsively that he

must find out, the girl's courage faltered. She turned back to the door as if about to leave.

Max detached himself from the art journalist who'd been babbling *sotto voce* this whole time, writing his feature out loud to get Max's editorial comments. Max reached the door just as the girl slipped out. He caught her by the sleeve. She jerked around in fright as he stepped out after her onto the sidewalk, letting the gallery door close behind him. It had grown bitterly cold. The cars rumbling past drove icy wind against him and the girl.

"I didn't mean to frighten you," he said in his friendliest voice.

"What? What do you want?"

It was starting to sleet with a fine mist that stung his forehead and cheeks. "I want you to come inside."

"Why?" Her eyes were wide as they looked at him, the pupils small, and Max wondered if she was high on something.

"We have food, you know. Near the back. And some wine if you're of age."

"I'm twenty," she said, sticking out her chin. She sounded maybe seventeen.

"Ah. There you are, then. We do have some non-alcoholic punch. It's very good."

"I..." She hesitated and he saw her eyes welling up, her chest start to jerk. She turned away from him.

"Do you have some personal connection with Mr. Lake or his paintings?"

The girl brought herself under control, turned her sleet-misted face to him again, and Max felt his heart tighten. If only he had had such a chance with his daughter, this last effort to pull her back from wherever it was she'd run off to...

"Is he...?" the girl said. "Mr. Lake. Is he here?"

Max cocked his head at her, recognizing that she hadn't answered his question. He decided not to push it. "No, he's not. He's said he might make if for the unveiling tonight, but with Emery, it's all, well, speculative."

To his surprise, she smiled. It made her look radiant. The sleet had accumulated to a fine sheen on her hair that seemed to sparkle in the streetlights. Had Lyssa been so perfect near the end? So vulnerable and open? In his dreams Max thought she was. The most painful thing, of course, was that Max had spent so long erasing the ugly last time he'd spent with her, all their quarreling, that his memories of Lyssa's face were blurry.

"That fits," the girl said quietly and laughed, a pained sound.

"What? That Mr. Lake is not here? Or that we don't know if he will be?"

"Both."

The wind gusted suddenly, blowing Max's own carefully-coiffed silver hair and he realized that he would look like a drenched rat soon if they didn't move this inside. He could feel the accumulating sleet on his face start to run.

"Won't you come in?" he said. "The food is really good. Think of it as dinner. Enjoy the paintings. We're going to unveil his latest at eight p.m., whether Emery is here or not."

"I know," the girl said quietly and the fear was suddenly back in her eyes.

"Is there a problem with that?"

"No. Of course not. Maybe. I just... I love Mr. Lake's work. I'm... I guess you could say I'm a fan, even though I've never had the money to actually *buy* his stuff. But his last series, the stuff he did, it scared me. It made me... I don't know if I want to see any more."

The words seemed to slip directly into Max's head somehow, to rattle around in his brain, and unsettle him. Which made no sense, because not only was he getting cold and impatient, but Max *knew* all of Emery Lake's paintings, the whys and wherefores, at least as much as Emery had been able to explain them to him. So Max understood. And yes, there was tragedy, but that wasn't all there was. Not by half.

Without thinking, he found himself grabbing the girl's hands and holding them tightly. "You *must* come inside," he said, struggling to sound friendly, rather than desperate. "Let me give you some food, then let me take you from painting to painting, even the scary ones, and tell you what I know of them. The real story. I think that you need to know."

He saw her take a deep breath and felt the shudder that ran through her. But she didn't pull her hands back. And just holding her gloved hands in his, Max felt so warmed that for a moment he didn't care that he was getting drenched on this most important of nights.

"Alight," she said.

"Good. Good!" He pulled her after him

into the warmth, into the smell of people and of bouchées of curried chicken with diced mango, tartlets of sundried tomato with olive tapanade, proscuitto-wrapped asparagus spears, avocado slivers on crackers, crostinis of chimichurri beef with spicy Argentinian parsley sauce and roasted red peppers and Queso Fresco, roasted pumpkin and coconut soup in the back for the truly hungry. The clink of glasses. The hum of people discussing art, Emery's art, in Max's gallery.

With a sigh of relief, Max released her and shook himself off, careful not to touch his hair. He began to brush off the girl's shoulders too before he caught himself and stopped.

"First let's get you comfortable," he said.

He walked her to the coat check where he helped her out of her jacket and gloves, the ski hat still stuffed in the bomber jacket's pocket. Underneath, above the jeans and black army boots, she actually wore a very chic, black chiffon number that made her look older than he'd thought. Maybe twenty after all. Yet it also highlighted the white luminescence of her skin and the dark mascara she wore around those watchful eyes. The frightened animal. As desperate as Lyssa had been.

Steady, Max.

"My name, by the way, is Max Hebbler," he said and extended his wet hand again.

She took it lightly. "Like Hebbler of The Hebbler Gallery?"

"The same. And you are?" He held his breath, half-expecting her to say, *Lyssa, of course. Don't you recognize me, father?*

"Amy."

"Amy with a last name?"

She gave a half smile. "Just Amy."

"Alright, Just Amy. Do you want some food first, or shall we start with the paintings?"

"Food later. Paintings now. With stories about why he painted them like he did, right? Especially the scary ones."

"'The Death Cycle.'"

She shivered. "Is that what he called it?"

Max shook his head and glanced at his watch, wiped off beads of water. "It's what I call it. And you know what? I think if it's really those that bother you, we should start there. So you'll actually have a chance to understand before the unveiling."

He saw her swallow and nod. "Can I get a

drink first?"

Max looked hard at her. Something in the way she said that reminded him of Emery's bad times. And Lyssa's. But he nonetheless nodded and led her over to the punch and waited for her to fill her glass.

Then, reflecting on all that he had to tell her and how impossible it was that she would ever believe him, much less understand as Max did, more with his heart than his head, he asked the wine steward to pour him a tall glass of the fine Beaujolais he'd ordered for this event.

When he had it in his hand and Amy had refilled her punch glass, he led her towards the back of the gallery and the disturbing series of paintings showing various scenes of apocalypse. There was one of dogs ravaging a child. One where townspeople had gone mad and were burning their own houses. Each still had Emery's usual transcendent human figure in them, but in each, that figure was being buried under the larger masses of dark imagery. Overwhelmed.

Small wonder that these were the only paintings Max hadn't had to beg and borrow for tonight's retrospective. Only two of the death cycle paintings had actually been sold. People admired them, usually in a hand-to-the-throat sort of way, but no one wanted one of them hanging in their home.

Now Amy stood before them and he could see her own hands shaking as she brought them together to clasp in front of her. Maybe, Max mused uncomfortably, he should post a warning sign before this rear part of the gallery: *Warning! Emotionally-secure patrons only! Extended viewing may cause despair!*

"What...what caused him to do this?" Amy said now, her voice barely a whisper. She was focused on the Sally Anne painting. The glowing nurse tending the sick and dying. A nuclear winter rose in the background.

Max stood before her, smiling tightly. "You know who his usual transcendent figure is, don't you?"

"His wife."

"Mathilde Guillaume. That's right. They married when he was only twenty-two and still painting science fiction and fantasy covers. She was a flautist with the New York Philharmonic, but also a figure model. At least she was for Emery."

Amy had moved closer to him, unable to

take her eyes off the existential anguish of the painting yet apparently needing Max's damp warmth or presence to reassure her. It made Max feel young again. Strong and sure. He wanted to put an arm around the girl's shoulders but he restrained himself as she seemed to shrink even further before the painting, her voice coming out as barely a whisper.

"She died, didn't she? The papers didn't say how."

"Lung cancer," Max said, just as quietly. "Like a nuclear winter. These were all painted before she died. And then—"

"Oh my god." She finally looked up at him and the fear was so intense her eyes had welled up. "And then he finished just one more work? The one you're unveiling tonight?"

She backed away from him, heading left into the north atrium where they'd had to specially raise the roof to accommodate the huge, crated work that not even Max had seen, on his promise to Emery. The crate stood on a knee-high plaster pedestal that stretched side-to-side just shy of the work's twenty-seven foot span, and was spotlit right now in soft blue and amber lights.

Amy began circling it, looking up at its imposing height with her mouth open.

And for the first time that evening, Max hesitated. Because the power of Emery's works to move people, while it made for good business and publicity for the gallery, might be too much on this night. For this young art lover, at least.

Max thought he knew what the newest painting would express. What it *had* to express after the bizarre narrative Emery had delivered with it. But what if he was wrong? Could he really risk showing Amy something that might be the last little shove she needed to destroy what was obviously a rather precarious emotional stability? It would perhaps be better to just send her home.

He should forget telling a story she wouldn't believe anyway. Forget the foolish desire to be her surrogate father, to have a second chance to save Max's own daughter by proxy.

Just *send her home*.

Yet even as he stepped to intercept her where she was now backing away from the display, she spun around on him with eyes so wide and panicky he found himself reflexively holding out his arms to her.

She didn't fold herself into him, but she did grab his hands with her own and shook them. "Tell me!" she demanded. "Tell me what happened to him!"

So he did.

Available in trade paper and electronic form through Amazon, Barnes & Noble, Kobo, and wherever fine books are sold.